Destiny's FRENEMIES

Look for these and other books about Linelle Destiny in the Linelle Destiny Series:

Visit www.thesecretsistersclub.com

Linelle Destiny Series

Destiny's FRENEMIES

Dr. Alicia Holland
Illustrations by Anoop PC

This book may be ordered through booksellers or by contacting:

iGlobal Educational Services, LLC
PO Box 94224
Phoenix, AZ 85070
www.iglobaleducation.com
512-761-5898

Because of the dynamic nature of the Internet, any web addresses or links contained in this book may have changed since publication and may no longer be valid. The views expressed in this work are solely those of the author and do not necessarily reflect the views of the publisher, and the publisher hereby disclaims any responsibility for them.

This is a work of fiction. Names, characters, businesses, places, events, and incidents are either the products of the author's imagination or used in a fictitious manner. Any resemblance to actual persons, living or dead, or actual events is purely coincidental.

Linelle Destiny Series: **Destiny's Frenemies**

ISBN-13: 978-1-944346-16-4

Acknowledgements

I want to first honor God for placing in my heart to share my story with others. It was He whom brought Karen and I together to manifest this project. I am so grateful for Karen Hendry as she took my notes and helped write this fictitious book. There are truly no words to express my gratitude as you are truly a blessing.

I also want to thank Surendra Gupta for his creativity in formatting and Anoop PC for his creativity in bringing life to the designs and illustrations in this book series. Both of you are amazing!

Dedication

I dedicate this book series to my beautiful and talented daughters, Georgia and Amaiya Johnson. Remember, you are valued, loved, and competent. You are worthy!

Part 1
End of School

Chapter 1
School Year Ends

Finally! The school year is nearly done. It is Thursday and Destiny just has to get through this last couple of days and she is free! Of course, she absolutely loves her students and her job, but a break would be very nice. Besides, being away from school for the summer will give her a chance to focus on her tutoring business. It has been growing like crazy and she needs to consider her next move.

On her way out of the school at the end of the day, Destiny passes Julie's classroom. She pops inside to say hi and ask Julie what her plans are. Destiny is hoping Julie will want to get together during the summer to do something fun. Destiny has no idea what that might be, but she is up for some adventure.

When Destiny peeks inside the classroom, she finds a scene that confuses her. Julie has a box sitting on her desk and she is packing it. What on earth is Julie packing? She shouldn't need to change anything in her classroom. Then Destiny notices the tears streaming down Julie's cheeks. She knows something big is up and steps inside the classroom.

Since the students are gone for the day, the school is quiet and Destiny and Julie are alone. "Hey, Julie," says Destiny. She can see that Julie is packing her personal things and clearing out her desk.

Julie looks up. "Oh, I didn't hear you come in," she says, wiping the tears from her face.

"What's going on?" asks Destiny. "Why are you packing your things?"

Julie looks at Destiny briefly and there is a lot of hurt in her eyes. "Because the powers that be have seen fit to demote me." She goes back to packing.

"What?" says Destiny. "I don't understand."

"I've been demoted and I'm no longer needed in as an ESL teacher."

"What? But why?"

Julie says nothing in response. She doesn't even look up. She just keeps putting things in the box.

Destiny takes Julie's coldness as a sign of how upset she is about the situation. "I mean, you have been great here. Just look at what you have done for the ESL program. You have improved it by leaps and bounds. How on earth could they possibly demote you?"

"Well, apparently, I have not been getting the results they expected of me this past year. Plus, there are cutbacks, so Easton says, but I don't know. They were able to hire you."

There is an edge to Julie's voice as she says this last bit. Destiny chooses to ignore it. She is certain Julie's tone is only because she is upset. "But you're not leaving, are you?" asks Destiny.

"No," says Julie in a too-cheerful voice. "No, it's far better than that. I get to stay on as an ESL teacher's aide. Isn't that great?"

"Oh. Oh, I'm so sorry, Julie. I…"

"Don't worry about it," says Julie. "At least now there is a classroom freed up for someone. Maybe they'll hire someone else who will need a classroom."

"What?" says Destiny.

"Well, the principal's pet needed to have her own classroom, didn't she? And Mal's was freed up. Maybe someone new is coming in and needs this one."

Destiny is stunned and deeply hurt by Julie's words. She doesn't know what to say and she doesn't know why Julie is speaking to her this way. When Mal was let go, Julie would always say Mal did it to herself. It takes Destiny a moment to respond.

"That's not fair," Destiny finally says.

"Isn't it? Seriously, Easton loves you and the chance to give you a classroom of your own meant someone had to go. Now, maybe another new teacher is coming and someone else has to go. I guess that someone is me."

Julie goes back to packing her belongings and Destiny just stands there with her mouth hanging open, completely speechless.

"I never wanted to get a classroom that way. I mean, sure I wanted one. Who wouldn't? But I didn't want to see anyone hurt just so I could have my own classroom. And this has nothing to do with me. You know that."

"Do I?" Julie says without looking up.

Destiny doesn't know what else to say. After a moment, she turns and walks out of the classroom. She walks straight past the elevator and takes the stairs. Halfway down to the next floor, Destiny sits on one of the steps and begins to cry.

How could Julie say those awful things? Destiny thinks about it. Destiny has worked hard for what she has achieved and she has never wished ill of any of her colleagues. Destiny does not want any of her success to come at the expense of anyone else.

The way Julie treated her reminds Destiny of Haley Davis, the girl she went to high school with and who treated her badly. Haley only wanted to be friends with Destiny in so much as it would help her get ahead. In the end, Haley was nothing more than bad news.

Then Destiny realizes what this situation truly means for her. It isn't what Julie said about the classroom, but how easily she can be pushed aside at the whim of Principal Easton. What he did to Mal and Julie is something he can do to anyone at any time.

Destiny has a feeling, deep within her soul that something is very wrong with this situation. Principal Easton isn't the person she thought he was and he isn't the leader she thought he was. He isn't a leader that can speak life into others and that is what Destiny needs in her life. She needs someone who doesn't play favorites and can change favorites on a dime.

Destiny hears a door open above her and someone starts walking down the stairs. She gets up, wipes her tears away, and begins to walk downstairs. She resolves that from now on she will pay very close attention to what is going on around her and listen to her own voice.

On the drive home, Destiny realizes that she needs to look for another teaching job at a different school. She would prefer to teach younger kids anyway and she wants to go to a school in which she can thrive under a leader that will help nurture her career without taking from others.

When she gets home, Destiny immediately sits down at her computer and pulls up the school board website. There are a few jobs available for the following school year and Destiny takes her time browsing through them, thoroughly digesting the information from each and every posting.

There is one position that stands out for her, a position teaching a grade five class. That sounds like a lot of fun and Destiny decides she will apply for it. However, she doesn't limit herself. The grade five position is her preference, but she applies for a few others, as well. She absolutely cannot stay where she is because she will not tolerate getting ahead at the expense of others and she won't work in a place where she always has to look over her shoulder for fear of losing her job to a new favorite.

It takes Destiny an hour and a half to submit applications for each of the jobs for which she is applying. When she is done, she stands up, stretches, and feels very satisfied with what she has done. She is going to look out for herself by making sure she is in a work environment that is healthy, not the toxic one in which she currently works.

With her stomach rumbling with hunger, Destiny goes to make herself some dinner. It's now time to leave her future in God's hands.

Chapter 2

Last Day

The next day is the last day of school for the year. Destiny has mixed emotions after her talk with Julie yesterday. Their school assembly is first thing in the morning and Destiny walks into the gymnasium with her class. Other classes are filing in and Destiny sees Julie standing on the far side of the gym, her arms crossed in front of her, looking very uncomfortable. Destiny considers going over to her, but decides against it and sits down along the side by her class.

The assembly gets started with the grade four class singing a song. Then Principal Easton gets up and says a few things. The assembly goes on for a while, with Principal Easton and the various teachers handing out student awards. Then Principal Easton gets up and says, "And now we have our final award of the morning, the Teacher of the Year Award. This is a special honor this year because it is a teacher that just joined us."

Destiny had been watching her students, proud of their accomplishments, when she hears Principal Easton and looks up to the front. She is the only new teacher in the school this year, but how could she get Teacher of the Year after just a year? It can't be her.

"This teacher is only in her first year of full-time teaching, which makes this accomplishment all the more impressive. She has done wonders with her students and her foray into teaching has been a true inspiration to us all. Miss Sycamores, would you please come on up?"

Destiny is stunned. She gets up and goes to the front of the gym amidst loud cheers and whoops, mostly from her students, who are definitely louder than anyone else.

When everyone quiets down, Destiny says, "Thank you so very much, everyone. I am so thrilled and honored, but I definitely did not accomplish this alone. I want to thank my students because they make teaching such an immense pleasure."

Loud cheers erupt from the students Destiny has been teaching all year. "And I want to thank three other special people. First, Principal Easton, thank you for giving me the opportunity to teach at this wonderful school."

There is a lot of clapping and Principal Easton says, "Thank you."

"And thank you so much to Miss Yonso and Miss Davis, who took me under their wing and helped me adjust and find my way around this massive school." Laughter from everyone. Katie looks grateful for the mention, but Julie looks far from impressed.

"Anyway, thank you to everyone for all your support." Destiny takes her seat, feeling so happy. She is in heaven throughout the rest of the assembly. When the assembly is over, many people gather around and congratulate Destiny. Katie comes running up and gives her a big hug. "I'm so happy for you!" she says.

But Julie just walks past Destiny without saying a word. Destiny watches as she disappears down the hall. "Don't worry about her," says Katie, touching Destiny's arm. "She'll come around."

Destiny nods her head, but she isn't so sure. More people congratulate her on the way out of the gym and Destiny realizes nothing can bring her down today.

Later that day, the class is chattering away, clearly excited that it is the last day of school. As long as the noise level stays reasonable, she lets them talk as she packs up her things and gets ready to leave. She wants to go just as much as they do—well almost.

Then the bell rings. Destiny says, "Goodbye, everyone! Have a great summer!" She expects a mass exodus, but a few of the kids come up to her desk.

"Hi guys," says Destiny.

"Hi, Miss Sycamores," says Jake. "We just wanted to say goodbye to you and give you a few gifts."

They place some wrapped packages and gift bags on Destiny's desk.

"You are the best teacher ever," says Tiffany. "Thanks for helping us understand math better."

Destiny is touched. "Thank you so much, all of you. But you are all smart kids. You just needed someone to help you see that."

"Well, thanks and thanks for coming to our games," says Jake. Then the kids grab their bags and leave, whooping as they get out into the hallway. Destiny should go quiet them down, but she lets them have their moment.

A minute later, as Destiny is putting the gifts from her students in a plastic bag she had tucked in her desk, Katie comes in.

"Hey, girl," says Katie. "Look at all that loot. The kids love you, you know."

"I guess they do," says Destiny.

"Yup, which is why I came to ask a favor."

Destiny looks at Katie and can see the question in her eyes. "Oh yeah?" she says.

"Would you be able to help out with the summer program and some math tutoring this year?" asks Katie. "I know you have your tutoring business and it's summer and all, but there is no one who can get through to the kids like you can."

"Thanks for the flattery," says Destiny with a wink, "but I would have said yes anyway."

"Well, it's the truth. You just know how to reach the kids, especially the ones who are struggling. And thanks. I knew I could count on you."

"You sure can. But I want to have some adventure this summer, too. You game?"

"Sure am," says Katie.

"I just wish Julie was on board," says Destiny. "I don't think she'll ever talk to me again."

"Sure she will," says Katie. "Just give her time."

"Yeah," says Destiny, not really believing it. "Walk out with me?"

"Sure," says Katie.

They leave the classroom and Destiny shuts the door behind her. Let the summer begin!

Destiny pulls out of the parking lot a few minutes later and heads into town. She has decided she deserves to treat herself to a nice dinner out to celebrate the end of her first year of teaching and her award. She asked Katie to join her, but Katie already had plans, so Destiny is on her own.

That's fine because she wants to start making plans for the summer. She finds a nice Louisiana-style restaurant and goes in. The waitress that meets her at the door says, "Hi. For one?"

"Yes, please," says Destiny.

She is given a nice little table near the window and orders an ice tea. As she looks at the menu, she considers what her summer will be like. When the waitress comes back with her drink, Destiny says, "I will have the Shrimp Malacca."

"Good choice," says the waitress.

"Well, I'm celebrating the end of the school year."

"Sounds good. Shouldn't be too long. We're not busy right now."

"Thanks," says Destiny, as the waitress takes her menu and leaves the table.

Then Destiny pulls out her planner and starts looking at the dates. The summer program doesn't start for two weeks, so she has some down time. And the tutoring center can get by without her for those two weeks. Not as many students com in the first half of the summer. That would be a great time to go home for a visit.

Then, when she gets back from visiting her family, Destiny can start considering plans to expand her tutoring business. After all, business is booming and she needs to have a central location from which to operate her center. Having everyone come to her will make it much easier to help more kids.

Destiny is putting her planner away just as her food arrives. The Shrimp Malacca is steaming hot and smells so good. It's been ages since Destiny has had it.

"Enjoy," says the waitress.

Destiny says, "Thanks!" Then she digs in. What a summer this will be!

Chapter 3
Office Space

Destiny opens her bleary eyes. What is that noise? She was having such a nice dream in which she was running her tutoring center and it was huge. There were so many students and she had Alvin helping her and other employees to ensure things were running smoothly.

It takes Destiny a moment to realize the noise that woke her up is the ringing of her telephone in the living room. Destiny turns her head to look at the clock on her nightstand. 8:45 am. Well, so much for sleeping in today.

Destiny slips out of bed and hurries out to answer the phone before it stops ringing.

"Hello," she says, hoping she doesn't sound sleepy.

"Hello, Destiny. It's Nichole Mayweather. We met a couple of weeks ago regarding office space for your tutoring center?"

"Hi, yes," says Destiny. "It's good to hear from you."

"I hope I'm not getting you out of bed," says Nichole.

"No, not at all." Destiny lies through her teeth, but she is desperate for some good office space and she wants to make the most of what Nichole has to offer.

"Wonderful! I have been thinking about your needs and I have an offer that I don't think you can refuse."

"Really," says Destiny, sitting down at her desk. "What is it?"

"Oh, I can't just tell you. I have to show you. But I *can* tell you this offer will allow you to expand your tutoring business in a fabulous office space."

"Sounds pretty good so far."

"Can you meet me at my office?" asks Nichole. "Say 1:30?"

"Yes, I can be there," answers Destiny.

"Wonderful! I'll see you then."

"Okay, see you then," says Destiny. "Bye."

After she hangs up, Destiny sits there for a moment. Then she realizes how exciting this is. She is about to expand her tutoring business, something she started doing when she was in high school. What a momentous day this will be!

At 1:25, Destiny pulls into a parking space just half a block from Nichole's office. It's a tight squeeze for her big truck, but there aren't any other parking spots nearby, so Destiny makes the spot work.

By 1:30, Destiny is walking through the door to Nichole's office. She can see that Nichole is finishing up with a client, so she sits in the waiting area and browses through a recent issue of Better Homes and Gardens magazine.

About five minutes later, Nichole sees her client out the door. As she walks over, Destiny stands up.

"Hi, Destiny. So sorry to make you wait."

"That's fine," says Destiny. "I was enjoying the photos of the homes in the magazine."

"They do have some gorgeous homes in there, don't they?"

Destiny nods.

"Well, follow me," says Nichole. "I have something to show you."

Destiny expected them to leave the office and drive to another location, so she is incredibly intrigued when Nichole leads her to a door at the back of the reception area. They enter the room beyond and Destiny sees that it is a large room with a couple of long tables. There are chairs at the tables, a nice book shelf at the back of the room, and a washroom off to one side.

"Well, what do you think?" asks Nichole.

"It's a great space," says Destiny.

"Great for a tutoring center, don't you think?"

"Well, yes, it would be."

"I'd like to rent it to you, if you're interested. It would be perfect! Most of your business goes on outside of regular business hours, so there would be very little overlap between our respective clientele. Plus, you would have a reception area, so parents could wait in comfort if they wish to stay while their child is being tutored."

Destiny is stunned. "The space is perfect! Yes, I would love to, but of course, it would depend on the rent. The business is still relatively small."

"Oh, don't you worry about that," says Nichole. "I'll keep it very reasonable for you. I know you are just starting to really grow. Plus, I want to sign my son, Charlie, up to get help from you. If you're here, it will make it easy for me to get him to your center. It's a win-win!"

"It sure is," says Destiny. "Thank you so much."

"I'll draw up a lease and bring it over to you tomorrow. We can finalize the details and then you can set up shop, notify your clients, and start advertising."

"That sounds great," says Destiny. The two women walk back out to the reception area.

"So, I'll see you tomorrow," says Nichole. "I am sorry to rush, but I have a house to show in a half an hour and it's on the other side of town."

"No problem," says Destiny. "I'll see you tomorrow."

They shake hands and Destiny walks out into the afternoon sun.

Destiny pulls into her parking lot at home, thrilled with how her summer has begun. A relaxing weekend, followed by an offer she truly couldn't refuse.

As she unlocks her apartment door, Destiny realizes how fortunate she is to have Nichole in her life. She also thinks about her interactions with Nichole. They are so professional, but also respectful. It is clear that Nichole has respect for Destiny's skill, experience, education, and expertise and she can sense that respect every time they meet.

Destiny thinks about her relationships at school, while she fills the kettle with water and sets it on the stove. She has never felt that level of respect with any of her relationships at work, not with Principal Easton or any of her colleagues. Not even conversations with Julie or Katie have ever felt like what she has with Nichole.

Where Nichole is supportive, the others are ready to stab each other in the back if it helps them further their career. And when someone accomplishes something, they receive nothing but false congratulations to their face and whispers and rumors behind their back. And it's not just her experience with getting a classroom and being awarded teacher of the year. Destiny has heard this kind of talk about others go around the school and it's nasty.

At least Julie isn't going behind Destiny's back. While it may not be justified, Julie isn't pretending to be happy for Destiny, while talking about her behind her back. She is just up front upset.

Even Principal Easton is far from supportive. He seems to play favorites, apparently with those who will make him and his school look better, rather than offering his staff the support they need to do their very best. Destiny might be in his favor now, but she knows this could change on a dime.

Destiny sighs contentedly as she pours a cup of tea. At least she is doing what she needs to do to take care of herself. She sits at her kitchen table and smiles as she sips her tea. Thank goodness she applied for a new teaching position. It was a good move. Destiny knows that deep down and she knows that things are about to get a whole lot better both at school and with her tutoring business.

Part 2
Summer

Chapter 4

A Growing Business

On Thursday afternoon there is a knock at Destiny's door. Destiny opens it and says, "Right on time."

Katie comes in, all smiles. "I'm always on time. You know that."

"Yes, I do. Come on in. Would you like a cup of tea?"

"Yes, please."

Destiny puts the kettle on and sets a teapot on the counter and cups on the table. She also sets out a plate of homemade chocolate chip cookies. Katie looks at the plate and grimaces. "It's hard to diet when you put that in front of me."

"Sorry," says Destiny, about to take the cookies off the table.

"Oh, no," says Katie, putting her hand on Destiny's. "I'm sure just one or two won't hurt."

Destiny laughs. "Not at all."

The friends chat about the summer program while Destiny makes tea. Destiny brings the pot of tea to the table with the cups and chuckles when she sees how many cookies Katie has eaten.

"How many's that? Four?"

Katie frowns. "Who's counting?"

They pour their tea and Destiny sighs.

"What's that about?" asks Katie.

"I don't know. Things seem different still, you and I getting together, but not with Julie."

"I know."

"Have you heard from her?"

Katie looks at Destiny over the rim of her cup. "Yeah, I saw her yesterday."

"How is she?"

"She's fine."

"Did she say anything about me?" asks Destiny. "I mean, does she seem less angry?"

"No, sorry. She's still angry and she thinks you took what was hers."

"Well, I did," says Destiny.

"What? No you didn't."

"Well, yeah, I did," says Destiny. "I mean, I didn't mean to. I didn't go looking for it, but Principal Easton chose me to be his golden teacher and Julie paid the price. I could have said no."

"No," says Katie. "No, you couldn't. That would have been career suicide."

"Well, I think it's career suicide to stay at that school with Principal Easton. I mean, sure, he favors me now, but that will wear off and then I'll be just as expendable as Julie."

"No way," says Katie.

"Yes, which is why I'm looking for another job."

"What? Really? Where?"

Destiny chuckles. "I applied for a few positions. Haven't heard anything yet, but I hope something pans out. Plus, I have my tutoring business and it has been growing like crazy."

"Oh, yeah?"

"I'm going to be renting some office space. The new tutoring center opens on Saturday."

Katie whistles. "When you mean business, you mean business," she says.

"Oh, it's wonderful, Katie. It's just the right size for my growing student base. I love it."

"Well, if anyone can pull it off, I mean running a thriving tutoring center and teaching full-time, it's you. I think it's great."

"You mean that?"

"Sure I do. When you get all set up, I'll have to come and see it."

Destiny smiles and their conversation turns back to the summer program and summer plans to have some fun and see their families.

The next day, Destiny walks into Nichole's office, which is also now her office, carrying a few bags full of supplies, books, and visual aids. Nichole is at the desk and she looks up when Destiny walks in.

"Hi there," says Nichole.

"Hey, Nichole."

"Listen, Charlie is in there. I thought he could talk to you about what he struggles with in math, you know, so you can get a feel for it. And also to make him feel better. He is nervous about school next year. If he knows you can help him, you know, before the school year starts, it'll make a world of difference."

"Sure thing, Nichole."

"Thanks!"

Destiny goes back and sees Charlie sitting at the table farthest from the door, reading a comic book.

"Hi," says Destiny, walking up to the table and setting her bags on it. "You must be Charlie."

Charlie nods.

Destiny sits down next to Charlie and says, "Your mom says you're concerned about math next year."

Charlie nods again.

"What has you so concerned?"

"Fractions," says Charlie.

"I see. You have a hard time with fractions?"

Charlie nods a third time and says, "I hate fractions, especially adding and subtracting them."

"Well, I don't know that fractions deserve that much wrath," says Destiny with a smile. "I'll tell you what. When you come in on Saturday, I'll show you a few tricks you can use to conquer those fractions. You might not end up liking them, but you will be able to add and subtract them pretty easily by the end of the summer. We can even look at what you might need to know for next year, get a jump on it. How does that sound?"

"That sounds great," says Charlie.

"How about you help me with what's in these bags," says Destiny, standing up and passing one to Charlie. "I need to get this stuff organized, and I suspect you have to wait for your mom, anyway."

"Okay."

"You can stack those visual aids on the shelf over there, while I sort out these supplies."

Charlie walks over to the shelf and opens the bag. Destiny watches as he starts taking things out and when he sees some visual aids with fractions, he stops and looks at them. She can see he is thinking long and hard about it. Then he nods his head and keeps putting things on the shelf.

Destiny looks over at the door and sees Nichole watching. She winks at Nichole and Nichole smiles. Charlie will be just fine.

Summer passes quickly once the tutoring center opens and the summer program is in full-swing. One Saturday morning in early August, Destiny is sitting at her desk in the center, looking at her numbers. She is stunned at how much her center has grown.

Nichole pops her head in. "Hey there. I'm going to the diner for some lunch. You want anything?"

"No thanks," Destiny answers, still staring at her enrolment numbers.

"Everything okay?" asks Nichole.

"Okay? Everything is great. I can't believe how much the center has grown!"

"I can. You are very good at what you do. Charlie is like a new kid."

Destiny feels her cheeks flush. "Thanks, but you have helped tremendously. I know you know a lot of people."

"Well, yes, I do, but I'm only telling them what I know. If you can help Charlie feel better about math, that is a feat. People need to know that so they can bring their kids to you. It's the least I can do after what you have done for Charlie."

"Well, I am very grateful."

"I guess that makes two of us," says Nichole. "You sure you don't want anything?"

"Maybe I'll walk over with you. I have some time before the center opens. Some fresh air might be nice."

Destiny and Nichole walk over to the diner, but Destiny feels as though she is soaring.

Chapter 5
Changing Tides

T he summer program is going well and Destiny is enjoying working with the students. The Thursday morning after the program starts, Destiny is in the office checking her mailbox when Principal Easton pops his head out of his office.

He spots her and his face lights up. "Destiny, can I see you for a moment?"

"Sure thing," says Destiny, heading for Principal Easton's office.

Once inside, Principal Easton motions for Destiny to sit down.

"I just wanted to discuss some changes I have been making to the teaching schedule," says Principal Easton and Destiny gets a sinking feeling in the pit of her stomach. Somehow, she already knows this can't be good.

"I have decided to appoint you as the Grade 6 math teacher. Your classroom will also change and you will be on the second floor, room," he pauses as he looks at a piece of paper on his desk. "215," he finishes and he looks up expectantly.

"Regular Grade 6?" asks Destiny. "But we already discussed this and you agreed to give me the Grade 6 advanced math. I don't understand."

"Yes, I know that's what we discussed, but things change on a dime in our schools. With new students coming and others leaving, our needs change. It turns out that this year I need you teaching the regular Grade 6 students."

"But what about the advanced students? Will we still have an advanced class? Who will be teaching that?"

Principal Easton stands up, an indication that he isn't going to discuss this any longer. "Nothing is carved in stone yet in terms of the advanced math, but you have your assignment so you can get yourself ready and settle into your new classroom."

"But..."

"I'm sorry, Destiny," says Principal Easton, "but I need to get to a meeting at the district office first thing this morning. I need to run."

The next thing Destiny knows, she is standing up and is being ushered out of Principal Easton's office. He shuts the door behind them and nods to her and then he's gone, leaving Destiny slightly stunned and very angry. Her blood is just boiling beneath her skin.

She definitely did the right thing applying for other teaching jobs and any doubts she might have had have been completely washed away. This is the exact same thing Principal Easton did to Julie. Promises were made and broken. She was shifted around, then she was demoted and ended up getting fired. Well, Destiny is not going to wait around and let that happen to her. She is watching her own back because no one else is going to do it. No one except for God.

The only thing that makes Destiny squirm a little is that she hasn't been accepted for any of the positions for which she applied. If she doesn't get accepted elsewhere, she will be stuck at the mercy of Principal Easton and the thought of that makes Destiny shiver.

Think positive thoughts, Destiny tells herself as she heads off to summer camp. But positive thoughts were hard to come by that day.

The day at summer camp went well, despite Destiny's mood and her concerns. Destiny unlocks her mailbox and pulls out her mail, happy to be home at the end of a long day. She sifts through the mail and finds a letter from the school board. Excitement shoots through her as she opens the letter on the spot. It reads:

Dear Miss Sycamores,

We are pleased to inform you that you have been accepted for a teaching position at Greenleaf Elementary School, effective August 1. Please fill out the attached paperwork and return it at your earliest convenience.

Destiny is jumping up and down as she reads the letter. This is it! She doesn't have to remain at the mercy of Principal Easton's whims. Plus she gets to teach elementary school kids, which is what she trained for and what she really wants to do.

"What has you so excited?" asks a voice from behind Destiny. She turns around to see Sharia standing there.

"Oh, I'm so happy, Sharia! I got a new teaching job, at Greenleaf Elementary!" Destiny waves the acceptance letter in the air in front of Sharia.

"That's great!" says Sharia. "I didn't realize you were looking for another position."

"Yeah, well, things aren't terribly stable where I am," says Destiny. "The Principal has his own plans and if you don't fit into them, then you don't last long."

Sharia nods. "I've seen that before," she says, pulling her mail out of her mailbox. "I'm glad you're getting out of there. You're too good of a teacher, and a person, to have to deal with any of that nonsense."

"Thank you," says Destiny, feeling touched that Sharia would say something so nice.

"I'm just tellin' it like it is. You deserve the new job."

"You're awesome," says Destiny, giving Sharia a big hug.

"Oh, honey, you know it!" says Sharia and they both laugh. "We need to celebrate you know."

"We will," says Destiny, as she starts up the stairs to her apartment. "Tomorrow!"

Sharia nods and Destiny feels relieved and happy.

As soon as Destiny gets inside her apartment she drops her bag at the door and heads over to her desk. Soon she has paper in front of her, a pen in her hand, and she begins to write her resignation letter.

Destiny decides she will personally deliver the letter to Principal Easton tomorrow. After all, there is no point in postponing the inevitable.

Destiny imagines the look on Principal Easton's face and giggles. It's really not nice of her to imagine him being so shocked and upset that she would dare leave his school, but she can't help it. Then again, maybe he'll be relieved that he doesn't have to do the dirty work of demoting her and eventually getting rid of her himself.

Who knows, thinks Destiny as she finishes her letter and signs it with a flourish. All she knows is that she is going to a better place. At least, she hopes so. Not every principal will be like Principal Easton.

Destiny folds the letter carefully and tucks it in an envelope. Then she writes Principal Easton's name on it and puts it in her bag so she won't forget it in the morning.

With a contented sigh, Destiny puts on some music and starts doing a little housework. She is just jiving along, happy as can be. Then she gets the leftover soup out of the refrigerator to warm it up for dinner. Tomorrow will be an exciting day and she can't wait!

Chapter 6
New School

Two weeks later, Destiny walks through the door of her new school, eager to get started. This school is a little smaller than the one she just left and that suits her fine. It will be easier to find her way around and maybe she won't get stuck in the elevator again.

Destiny turns left and enters the school office. The secretary isn't at her desk, but there is a woman standing behind the counter looking at some papers. She is short, well-dressed, and very neat-looking, her long golden blond hair falling in waves down her back. Destiny decides this must be Principal Limestone.

"Hello," says Destiny.

The woman looks up and her ruby red smile gives Destiny a shiver. "Oh, hi," she says. "You must be our new teacher, Miss Sycamores, is it?"

"Yes, but please call me Destiny."

"Pleasure, Destiny," the woman says, offering her hand to Destiny. "I am Daniella Limestone, Principal here at Greenleaf

Elementary School. Why don't you come right into my office so we can get acquainted?" Her Texan accent is thick and there is no doubt she was born and raised in this state.

They go into Principal Limestone's office and she offers Destiny a seat at a table in the corner of the room. Principal Limestone takes the other seat, pulls a folder toward her, and opens it up to look at Destiny's application for the teaching job.

"I must say," says Principal Limestone after a minute, "you seem very qualified. I am impressed with your accomplishments last year, it being your first year of teaching and all."

"Thank you," says Destiny. "I really am looking forward to working here though, with the grade five students."

"I am glad to hear that. They are an energetic bunch and they need some serious math help, but I have a feeling you'll do just fine by them."

"Well, I do love working with kids and helping them see math in a way they haven't before. Plus, I have a lot of experience. I've been tutoring since I was in high school."

"Yes, your tutoring background will be a great asset here. Do you have any questions for me at this point?"

"No, I don't believe so."

"Well, then," says Principal Limestone as she stands up, "why don't I show you to your new classroom."

Destiny nods her head and stands up and they leave Principal Limestone's office. In the main office, there is a short, round woman sitting behind the desk.

"Patti," says Principal Limestone, "this is our new teacher, Miss Destiny Sycamores."

"Nice to meet you, Destiny," says Patti.

"It's very nice to meet you, too," says Destiny in return.

"We are off to see Destiny's new classroom if anyone is looking for me," says Principal Limestone, not waiting for a reply. She walks out into the hallway, turns left, and Destiny follows. They walk until they come to a set of stairs and Destiny groans inwardly. Up I go again, she thinks.

But they only go up one floor and then they turn right and walk a short way down the hall. Principal Limestone stops in front of the second door on the left.

"Here it is," she says.

"Thank you, so much," says Destiny, entering the classroom. She is already looking around and deciding what she needs to get to make the classroom her own.

"I'll leave you to it, then," says Principal Limestone.

"Oh, yes. Thank you."

Then Destiny is alone and she sighs deeply, enjoying the moment before she sits at her desk and begins to plan her lessons.

Destiny stirs in her seat, feeling stiff. Then she looks at her watch and sees it is 11:48. No wonder, she thinks. She has been sitting working on her lesson plans for over two hours.

Destiny gets up and stretches and decides it is time to get some lunch. Since she wants to get to know the new neighborhood, she decided not to bring a lunch today. Surely there is a diner or restaurant nearby.

Out in the hallway, Destiny retraces her steps back to the stairs. In the stairwell, she meets a tall, blond woman who is also heading downstairs.

"Hi," says Destiny.

"Hello," says the woman. "You must be the new teacher."

"Yes. My name is Destiny. Destiny Sycamores."

"Hi Destiny. I'm Wendy Domino, science teacher here at Greenleaf." Wendy is very slim. Her fiery red hair, freckles, and green eyes somehow complement her casual dress, although Destiny can't imagine wearing jeans and a t-shirt to work.

"That's great," says Destiny as they reach the first floor. "I teach math, but the two subjects do go hand-in-hand. We should get together sometimes and see how we can coordinate our lesson plans. It always helps when students see the math they are learning in action."

"That's a great idea."

"So," says Destiny, "what's the school like? Do you like it here?"

"Oh, yes, I do, well the kids anyway. I'll be sad to leave them when the time comes."

"When the time comes for what?" asks Destiny.

"Well, I am planning to go to China. It's a dream I've had all my life, and soon I will take a trip there. Eventually, I want to live there, but it will all begin with a trip."

"That sounds great," says Destiny. "Why China?"

"Well, my boyfriend is from there and he is moving back. But I am also so done with this school system."

"Really? What do you mean?"

"There is just such a lack of support and it's so hard to get anywhere. I am not going to risk my career on the whims of the people in charge. But you've only been teaching here for a year, so maybe you haven't seen the dark side, yet."

"Actually," says Destiny, "I've seen more than enough."

"Then you get it."

"Yeah, I do," says Destiny.

"Well," says Wendy. "I have to run. I hope you aren't too discouraged. This school isn't bad, at least relatively speaking."

"No, I'm good," says Destiny.

"Enjoy the rest of your day," says Wendy with a wave as she speeds off down the hallway.

Destiny says goodbye and heads off to find a nice place for lunch. She is happy to have made a new teaching friend already.

It takes no time at all for Destiny to settle into her new teaching position. The kids in her class are great, although Principal Limestone wasn't kidding when she said they were energetic.

The fall has moved on and it's nearly the holidays. It is the last day of school, and as much as Destiny loves her work and her students, she can't wait to be done because she is going home to visit her family for Christmas.

As Destiny is finishing up a few things so she can head home for the day, she hears someone rush into her classroom.

"Guess what?" says Wendy, nearly shouting.

"What?" asks Destiny, looking up from what she is doing.

"I am doing it! I am going to China next year."

"Really?" says Destiny, running around her desk to give Wendy a hug. "Congratulations! I didn't think you were that close."

"Yes, I am. I am almost certain I have enough money tucked away and there are some really great travel deals coming along soon."

"Well, I'm really happy for you, Wendy."

"Thanks! Are you leaving now?"

"Yeah, just about. I have to get home and pack. I'm leaving first thing in the morning."

"Right, your trip home. Well," says Wendy, giving Destiny another hug, "have a fabulous time!"

"Oh, I will. And Merry Christmas."

"Merry Christmas to you, too!"

Wendy rushes out of the room and Destiny chuckles. Then she wraps up and heads home to pack. Excitement bubbles inside at the thought of seeing her family soon.

Part 3
Relationships

Chapter 7

Home for Christmas

The drive home to see her family was beautiful. It was nice to just be on the open road, no responsibilities, the weather sunny and lovely. Destiny left early in the morning to drive straight through. She didn't want to waste any time getting there because she is so eager to see her family. Apparently they are eager to see her, too, because as Destiny drives down her old street and pulls into her parents' driveway, everyone is waiting on the front step, smiling and waving as she parks her truck.

Destiny barely plants her feet on the ground when Momma is upon her, shouting, "My child, my child!" and nearly knocking Destiny over with the force of her hug.

Destiny is smiling and just soaking up Momma's love, and when Momma finally lets go, Destiny manages to shut the truck door before she is enveloped in the arms of her family in hug after hug.

"How was the drive down," asks Pop, Momma standing behind him, wiping the tears from her face and smiling, still saying, "My child," only more softly than before.

"It was just fine, Pop," says Destiny.

Destiny can see Pop looking her truck over with an approving nod. Then he turns to Dino and chuckles. "Dino, you got some work to do. Your sister done got you beat. Her truck is bigger than yours!"

"No way," says Dino, practically lifting Destiny off the ground in a huge embrace. "My little sister can't possibly own a bigger truck than mine! I think we gonna have to measure them to make sure."

"Oh, it's bigger," says Destiny with a wink to Pop.

"Well, we'll see about that," says Dino opening the truck door and taking out Destiny's suitcase. "Good Lord, what do you have in here, girl?"

"Clothes and a few presents," says Destiny.

"It feels like it's full of bricks." But Dino takes her suitcase up the steps and into the house.

Michelle gives Destiny a big hug and says, "It's so nice to have you home! I've missed you so much, we all have."

"I've missed you, too," says Destiny as she walks into the house with Michelle on one arm and Momma on the other. "Let's have some tea."

A couple of days later, Destiny is sitting in the bright, sunny kitchen eating breakfast when the doorbell rings. Destiny doesn't think anything of it until Momma calls in, "Destiny, it's for you."

Destiny's brow furrows. She is surprised that someone would be at the door for her. She didn't even know anyone other than her family knew she was home, and she has seen all of them. At least she is dressed, if only in sweats and a t-shirt.

Destiny puts her bowl in the sink and walks out into the hallway. There is Calix standing in the doorway. Destiny went to high school with Calix, which feels like a lifetime ago. It's been five years since she has seen him and he is as tall as she remembers, but definitely more muscular and very handsome.

"Hi Calix," says Destiny.

"Hi," says Calix, seeming a bit nervous.

"Well, I'll leave you two to catch up," says Momma. "This house ain't gonna clean itself. Never has!"

When Momma is gone, Calix says, "I hope you don't mind me dropping in like this. I heard you were in town for the holidays and thought it would be nice to see you."

"Thanks," says Destiny, a hint of confusion in her voice.

"Not many folks make it out of Many, Louisiana, so you're somewhat of a hero here, at least among our old classmates."

"Really?"

"Sure. Everyone wants to know how life is in Texas. Plus, I just thought it would be nice to see you, myself, you know?"

"Yeah, sure," says Destiny, not really sure at all of where this is leading.

"Well, listen," says Calix. "I can't stay too long because I have to run some errands for my momma, but can I get your phone number? I can call you and maybe we can go out sometime while you're here."

Destiny is stunned. Since when does Calix show any interest in her? "Sure," she says and gives him her number. He gives her his number and says goodbye. After she closes the door behind him, Destiny leans against it for a moment and a thrill runs through her. Huh, she thinks. Calix. Who would have known?

Christmas Day comes and goes and it is late evening on Boxing Day. Destiny comes in the door, just getting back from taking her nephews, Alex and Carlos, and their cousin Victoria to the movies. They went to see Fat Albert and it was so funny they spent the whole drive home still laughing about how funny it was. The boys were imitating Fat Albert from the back seat and Destiny and Victoria were giggling away up front.

When Destiny walks in the door, she looks at her cell phone and realizes she missed a call from Calix. Her phone was off during the movie and with the craziness of the holidays she had almost forgotten he was going to call.

Destiny goes into the living room, sits on the sofa, and calls Calix. He answers after the second ring and says, "Hi, Destiny."

"Hi," says Destiny. "I'm sorry I missed your call. I was at the movies with my nephews."

"No worries," says Calix. "Listen, I was wondering if you would like to go out tomorrow night. There are a bunch of us getting together to go out to dinner and dancing and they all want to see you again."

"Gee, that would be great, but I'm leaving first thing in the morning to go back to Texas."

"Oh, no," says Calix and Destiny can hear the disappointment in his voice.

"I'm so sorry it didn't work out," says Destiny, "but my tutoring center opens back up next week and I need to get back and get ready for that. Maybe we can get together the next time I'm in town."

"I understand. A successful gal like you has a busy schedule." Destiny can hear the teasing tone in his voice and breathes a sigh of relief that he's not upset with her.

"Ha ha," says Destiny. "Well, thanks for the invite and say hi to everyone for me."

"I will, and you have a safe trip back. Who knows, maybe if I ever get to Texas, I'll drop in for a visit."

"That would be great."

"I hope you mean that," says Calix and Destiny is sure he is teasing.

They say their goodbyes and Destiny smiles and she goes to pack up the last of her things for her drive home the next day. Unfortunately, the weather for her drive is supposed to be gloomy and wet, but at least her mood is sunny, having had a great family visit and having been asked out on a date by Calix!

Chapter 8

Test Time

O n the second day of school after the Christmas vacation, Destiny is feeling relaxed, thanks to the wonderful visit home to spend the holidays with her family. Feeling relaxed is a good thing because there are some big standardized tests being administered to the students in two weeks and Destiny is in charge of the math testing.

Thank goodness Destiny has had a break and a rest. She feels ready to take on the testing and she wonders if Wendy is ready. Destiny was so busy yesterday that she didn't get a chance to see Wendy. She is excited to touch base with her and tell her all about her holidays and being asked out by Calix. Maybe Wendy can go out for lunch with her today.

On the way up to her classroom that morning, Destiny stops by Wendy's room. She walks into the room, starts to say, "Hey there, Wen…" and stops short when she sees a new teacher sitting at Wendy's desk. "Oh, hi," Destiny says.

"Hi there," says the woman.

"Sorry, I was looking for Wendy. Is she sick today?"

"No, I believe she is away."

"Away?" says Destiny.

"I think so. I have been asked to fill in for at least the rest of this month."

"Oh, I see."

"Is there something I can help you with?" asks the teacher.

"Oh, no. It's just that, well, Wendy is a friend of mine. I was away over the holidays and didn't talk to her, so I didn't realize she had gone away."

"I see," says the woman, standing up and extending her hand. "Well, I am Stephanie Larkson and it looks like we'll be working together for at least a little while."

Destiny shakes Stephanie's hand. "Yes, it looks that way. I'm Destiny Sycamores, math teacher here."

"It's nice to meet you, Destiny," says Stephanie, who is very tall and slim, with a short dark bob and big silver earrings.

"You too," says Destiny. "Well, I had better get to my classroom and get ready for the day. I'll see you later."

"Okay, bye," says Stephanie, sitting back down and going back to her planning.

Destiny gets to her classroom and puts her things away, mulling over Wendy's absence as she does. She knew Wendy was going to China at some point, but Wendy made it sound like the trip was still months away. She didn't say anything about going over the holidays or that she would be gone so long. Why didn't she tell me, wonders Destiny.

Destiny sits down at her desk, thinking she should start getting a handle on what is involved with the testing so she is prepared when the time comes. But as she sifts through her mail, she finds two testing envelopes, one for math and one for science.

Surely this is a mistake because Destiny is only responsible for the math testing. Wendy would normally be in charge of the science testing, but since she isn't here, someone else will have to do it. Perhaps the science paperwork was accidentally put in her mailbox. The bell is due to ring in less than five minutes, so Destiny decides she will take the science envelope back down to the office at lunchtime. Then they can get it to the right teacher.

At lunch, Destiny heads down to the office, science envelope in hand. No one is in the main office, so Destiny pops her head into Principal Limestone's office. "Hi, Daniella."

"Oh, hi, Destiny. What can I do for you?"

"I just wanted to know whose mailbox to put the science test envelope in. It was put in mine by mistake."

Principal Limestone looks over the top of her glasses at Destiny. "Oh, that wasn't a mistake, dear."

"It wasn't?" asks Destiny stepping fully into Principal Limestone's office. "I don't understand."

"Well, Wendy is away, so we need someone to take charge of the science testing."

"Yes, I just found out about Wendy," says Destiny. "But surely someone else can take on the science, one of the other science teachers? I'll have my hands full with the math testing."

"Have a seat, Destiny."

Destiny hesitates and then sits down.

"Wendy's trip was somewhat unexpected. With her absence we all need to pitch in and pick up the slack."

"Of course," says Destiny, "I understand that, but like I said, wouldn't one of the other science teachers be better suited to take over the science testing?"

"No, I feel you are better suited. If you are doing the math testing anyway, adding the science only makes sense, particularly with your math skills. The science teachers have to pick up the slack in other ways while Wendy is gone."

"Even with the supply teacher here?"

"I'm afraid so."

Destiny thinks for a moment before responding. "Well, I'm not sure I can handle the additional work load. The math testing will be a huge responsibility on its own. I don't think I can do the science, too."

"Well, you'll have to."

"There is no other option? I mean surely we can work something out. Maybe two of the other science teachers can share it or something."

"Destiny, let me make this clear," says Principal Limestone. "I looked at this situation from every possible angle and you are the best one to take on the science testing. If you would rather not, I can find someone to replace you as the grade five math teacher. Otherwise, you need to fulfill your responsibilities."

Destiny is stunned. Principal Limestone just gave her an ultimatum. Take on the science testing or lose her job. Inside, Destiny is seething with anger, her stomach just knotting up, but on the outside she keeps calm and plasters a smile on her face.

"I see," she says. "Well, in that case, I guess I had better get to work."

"I'm glad you understand," says Principal Limestone as Destiny stands up, but Destiny doesn't understand at all. She doesn't understand why she seems to be the only one bearing the burden of Wendy's absence, despite what Principal Limestone has said about everyone chipping in to do their part.

Destiny says goodbye and walks out of the office, not speaking to anyone on the way. She walks straight out of the school and heads over to the diner for lunch. She considers taking her lunch back over and eating at her desk while she starts working on preparing for the testing, but she is too angry to be in the school right now and needs some time to cool down.

By the time she has finished lunch and paid her bill, she is feeling calmer and ready to face what she needs to face. However, she is concerned by what has happened and what it means for her future at this school. It seems that once again she is at the mercy of someone who will use her to suit their own purposes and Destiny doesn't want to be a puppet.

For now, Destiny will comply, but she needs to give some serious thought to her future and her career. She needs to start doing what is best for her.

Chapter 9
Calix

Destiny is snuggled up with a cup of tea. It is Saturday, February 13, and Destiny is beginning to wind down, thrilled that the month of January is behind her. The testing went relatively smoothly, or at least it appeared to on the surface. Behind the scenes, Destiny was scrambling to keep up with the administering and marking of all the tests.

Destiny is home for the evening. She is settled on the sofa, reading a recent paper on a new approach to tutoring when the phone rings. She picks up and says, "Hello."

"Destiny, hi!"

"Hi, Wendy," says Destiny, shocked to hear from her. It had been so long since she had seen Wendy.

"How are you?" asks Wendy.

"I'm just fine," says Destiny. "You?"

"I'm great! I just wanted to let you know I'm coming back to work next week and I have so much to tell you. Maybe we can do lunch on Monday?"

"Yeah, okay," says Destiny, feeling a little torn between happiness at finally hearing from Wendy and frustration with what Wendy left her and the school to deal with in her wake.

"Well, I have to go now," says Wendy, "but I'll see you next week!"

"Okay, bye," says Destiny, but as she hangs up the phone, Destiny can't help thinking, *It's about time you got back to your job and your responsibilities.*

Destiny turns her attention back to her paper, pushing thoughts of Wendy out of her mind. Hardly a minute later, the phone rings again. *That better not be Wendy again,* thinks Destiny. She has had her fill of Wendy's bubbly voice for one day.

"Hello," says Destiny.

"Hey, Destiny. It's me, Calix."

Destiny's heart races a little at the sound of his voice. "Hi, Calix. It's good to hear from you."

"I can do better than that," he says.

"Huh?"

"Go look out your window."

Confused, Destiny gets up and walks over to her living room window. She pushes aside the curtain and sees Calix standing in the parking lot, leaning up against his 1977 Cadillac, waving at her like a foolish schoolboy, a big grin on his face.

"Calix!" exclaims Destiny as she runs to the door, slips on her shoes, and shoots outside. "What are you doing here?"

"Just get down here and I'll tell you." And with that he hangs up.

Destiny reaches Calix a moment later, smiling from ear to ear. "What are you doing here?" she asks again.

"Well, it's Valentine's Day tomorrow and I'm here to take you to dinner."

"You drove all the way here to take me out for Valentine's Day?"

"Well, yeah. And I get to visit a friend while I'm at it. I'm staying at his place for the weekend. Two birds with one stone. Ya know?"

Destiny just stands there in awe.

"Well?" asks Calix.

"Well, yes!" says Destiny. After all, if the guy drove all this way to take her out, who is she to say no? He is definitely worth it!

"That's great! I'll pick you up at six o'clock and take you somewhere nice."

"Okay, see you then."

Destiny goes back inside, smiling the whole way. Yes, Calix is definitely worth it.

The following day, Calix is right on time and Destiny is waiting for him at the bottom of her stairs. He pulls up in front of her and she climbs into his big beast of a car. They drive for about 15 minutes, chatting about home and some of their old friends. Then they pull into the parking lot of Truluck's Seafood Restaurant, a place Destiny has never been.

Once inside and seated, they order drinks and then browse the menu. Destiny is silently stunned at the quality of restaurant to which Calix has brought her. It is all fine dining and candlelight. They decide they will order a combination seafood platter to share, but Destiny also orders crab cakes, her absolute favorite.

"Really?" asks Calix. "Crab cakes?"

"Can't live without 'em." Says Destiny.

Calix smiles and shakes his head.

"So you know what I've been up to," says Destiny. "What are you doing these days?"

"I work for a foundational drilling company. We drill holes for piers and build the foundations of big buildings, you know, like banks and hospitals and buildings like that."

"Sounds like tough work," says Destiny, sipping her ice tea.

"It is and it's okay, but what I really want to do is become a chef."

"Really? Why haven't you done it, yet?"

"Gotta save up the money, first," says Calix. "Chef school isn't cheap, so foundations it is, until I can afford school. I'm almost there," he adds with a smile.

"Well, I'm all work, what with my day job and the tutoring center."

"No one special in your life, then?"

Destiny can feel her cheeks flush. Is he really that interested? Then she remembers that he always has been, ever since she was in high school.

"No," Destiny answers. "I thought there was for a while, but he wasn't what I thought he was."

"Well, that's too bad for him, then, isn't it?" says Calix with a smile and a very mischievous look in his eyes.

Destiny's cheeks flush even more, and then their food arrives and they chat about all aspects of life. Destiny feels special and she really likes Calix. She is glad he didn't forget about her.

✧ ✧ ✧

On Monday morning, Destiny floats into school on a cloud of happiness. She is still flushed with the warm feeling of being with Calix for dinner the previous evening. She checks her mailbox, thinking she should go up and see Wendy, when she hears voices growing louder from Principal Limestone's office. One of the voices is Wendy's and Destiny wonders what is happening.

A few minutes later, while Destiny is sitting at her desk getting ready for her day, Wendy comes into the classroom. "Hey, Wendy," says Destiny. "How are you?"

"Hey," says Wendy. Then without an answer, she says "You know, I can't believe her."

"Who?"

"Daniella."

Destiny realizes that Wendy is really upset after her talk with Principal Limestone. "Why, what happened?"

"She is reading me the riot act for the time I took off. Honestly, I don't see what the big deal is. Teachers take time off all the time to go to Las Vegas and such. At least my trip had more meaning to it than a weekend of flashing lights and casinos."

"I get that," says Destiny, "but to be honest, Daniella isn't the person who really had to bear the brunt of your absence."

"What is that supposed to mean?" asks Wendy.

"Well," says Destiny. "I had to take over all your test-related duties and it was a lot of extra work. I was working 12- to 14-hour days just to keep up."

"Oh come on, Destiny. You work like that all the time. If it isn't your tutoring center it's some other professional development thing or something else. You're used to it and you came out the other side unscathed."

"It doesn't mean I should have had to do it, though."

"Well, blame Principal Limestone for not doing her job right and finding a suitable replacement."

And with that, Wendy is off to her classroom, leaving Destiny in disbelief. Can Wendy really be that oblivious to the bind she left everyone in? Destiny gets back to planning her day, trying to put Wendy out of her mind. At least Wendy is back now and Destiny can get back to her normal routine.

Chapter 10
Epilogue

T he weeks have gone on and April has arrived in a burst
of sunshine and flowers. The gardens are starting to get
dressed in their summer best. Destiny sees Wendy in the
hallway on the first Monday of April, walks up to her, and says
"Hi."

"Oh, hi." Wendy is short with Destiny. She has spoken with
Destiny less and less since their chat in February. Wendy has
clearly gotten the message that it wasn't just Principal Limestone
that had a problem with her time off work. A lot of teachers had
issues, whether they were directly affected like Destiny, or were
simply put off by the fact that Wendy got so much time off
during the school year, when she should have saved her trip for
summer vacation.

Destiny has been particularly frustrated because of the additional workload she had to take on, but she has been trying to
put that behind her and mend fences with Wendy. Wendy hasn't
made it very easy.

"Listen, I was wondering if you might want to catch lunch at the diner today," Destiny says.

"No, thanks," says Wendy. "I have things I have to do."

"OK," says Destiny. "I just haven't seen much of you and thought it would be nice to catch up."

"To be honest, I didn't really think you cared anymore."

"Wendy, that's not true and you know it!"

"Well, I'll be out of your hair soon enough, and everyone else's," says Wendy.

"What's that supposed to mean?"

"I'm resigning," says Wendy as she starts to walk away.

Destiny places her hand on Wendy's shoulder and Wendy stops walking. "Why on earth are you doing that?" asks Destiny.

"Because this is not the right environment for me. I cannot grow and thrive here like I want to and ever since my trip, everyone has been treating me like the bad guy. It's time for me to move on."

"Seriously? That's it? You aren't even going to finish out the school year?"

"Daniella already has my resignation and it's effective Friday."

And with that, Wendy walks off, leaving Destiny to watch her retreat down the hallway. Then Destiny looks at the mail in her hand. There is an official-looking envelope and she has a feeling she knows what's in it.

When she arrives in her classroom, Destiny opens the envelope and sighs with frustration. Sure enough, it's a letter from Principal Limestone, assigning Destiny all the science activities for grade five. Once again, Destiny has to bear the brunt of Wendy's poor decisions.

Destiny slams the paper down on her desk and takes a deep breath to calm her emotions before her students begin to arrive. However, as she acts to calm herself, she also realizes something incredibly important. She realizes on a whole new level that she needs to take charge of her life and her career.

There will always be drama in the workplace. Destiny sees that and knows she can't change it or hide from it. But she absolutely cannot just sit around waiting to be assigned work that really shouldn't be her responsibility. She cannot allow herself to be shuffled around at the whim of the principal simply because it is convenient.

This is Destiny's career. This is her life. And Destiny decides right then and there that she wants to be in charge of it and guide it wherever she wants it to go. That means doing whatever she can to make it better and letting go of what she can't change. It means having a good long think about where she wants to steer her career over the coming years.

The first of her students comes into the classroom. "Good morning, Miss Sycamore's," says Gerald.

"Morning, Gerald." Destiny tucks the letter in the top drawer of her desk as more students start to file in. *They are what really matters*, thinks Destiny, *and I'm going to make sure I do the very best for them and for me.*

About the Author

Alicia Linelle Holland was born and raised in Many, Louisiana and got her middle name after her mother, Vera Linelle. When Alicia was in middle school, she started the Secret Sister Club that you read about in the Linelle Destiny Book Series. Alicia Holland has been working towards bringing back the Secret Sister Club as she embarks upon quite an interesting life and spiritual journey. At age 26, she earned her Doctorate in Education so that she can be in a position to help others believe in themselves and go far. At age 31, Dr. Alicia Holland opened a Not for Profit, Alise Spiritual Healing & Wellness Center and was officially ordained as a Minister. As a Transformational Life Coach, Professor, Author, Speaker, and Minister, Dr. Holland travels the World sharing her message: "You are Loved, You are Valued, and You are Competent.

Dr. Alicia Holland has two beautiful daughters, ages 7 and 9, who travels the World with her and are active participants in the Secret Sister Club Mentoring Program. She and her family resides in Austin, Texas and are currently looking for a new puppy.

Dr. Holland is available for speaking engagements and can be reached at support@thesecretsistersclub.com or support@iglobaleducation.com.

www.ingramcontent.com/pod-product-compliance
Lightning Source LLC
Chambersburg PA
CBHW071207130626
46555CB00004B/1611